The Work Book
Everything Science

Marcia S. Freeman

Rourke
Publishing LLC
Vero Beach, Florida 32964

PHOTO CREDITS: Cover and pages 8, 9, 12, 14, 15, 18, 21, 22 © Lynn M. Stone; page 4 Picture Quest; pages 5, 6 Photodisc; page 10 © K-8; page 11 courtesy Fermi Labs; page 19 © Lois Nelson; page 20 © J. H. Carmichael; page 22 © Flanagan Publishing

Library of Congress Cataloging-in-Publication

Freeman, Marcia S.
   The work book (Everything science)

ISBN 1-59515-125-7

Printed in the USA

LK/BK

Table of Contents

What Is Work?

If something is moved—lifted or lowered, pushed or pulled, blown or washed—work is being done. That is the scientific meaning of work.

Two movers are doing work.

Working can also be fun.

Climbing a tree is work.

When you move yourself, you are doing work. Work, like swimming or hiking, can be fun.

Swimming is work.

Work Long Ago

   Long ago we used our own **muscles** to do most of our work. We also used animals to help us.

   We used the wind and **flowing** water to help us do work.

A windmill

A water mill

Long ago, we used horses for farm work. Today we use tractors.

People then **invented** all kinds of machines to help do work.

Today machines do much of our work. They remove snow from our roads and help us lift heavy loads.

Machines have helped make our work easier.

Animals and People Work

Around the world, people and animals still do a lot of the work.

Two young people do work on a farm.

This elephant's work is to move logs.

It takes **energy** to do work—to move things.

Where do animals get their energy to work?

Hint:

Carrying

Some animals carry things on their backs.
When an animal carries us, we call it a **steed**.

This horse is this man's steed.

When animals carry bundles of goods, we call them **beasts of burden**.

This camel is a beast of burden.

Pulling and Pushing

Animals are doing work when they move **vehicles**, tools, or machines.

They are doing work when they pull sleds or wagons.

These horses are working by pulling a sled.

If you push and pull a vacuum cleaner, you are doing work. You are moving something.

This girl is doing work when she moves the vacuum cleaner.

Working Insects

By moving this leaf, these ants are doing work.

Even insects do work. The ants in the picture are carrying a leaf piece from one place to another.

Worker bees carry **pollen** from flowers to their hive. They carry the pollen on their back legs.

The yellow powder on the bee's legs is pollen.

Who Is Working?

Animals and people work everywhere... on farms, in factories, on boats, at home, and in schools.

Carrying something is work.

Moving something is work.

Glossary

beasts of burden (BEESTS uv BURD un) — animals that
carry goods

energy (EN ur jee) — what is needed to make things go, run,
or happen

flowing (FLO ing) — moving in a stream, like water

invented (in VENT ud) — thought up or made

muscles (MUS ulz) — body parts that can contract and expand to
produce movement

pollen (POL un) — grainy powder from small stalks inside
a blossom

steed (STEED) — an animal that is ridden

vehicles (VEE uh kulz) — any machines like cars, sleds, and
bikes that carry people or things

Index

Science Standard: Forces and Motion
When things are moved, work is done.

Marcia S. Freeman loves writing science books for children. A Cornell University graduate, she has taught science and writing to students from elementary to high school, and their teachers too! Her 50 books also include children's fiction and writing education texts for teachers.